Grannies and other Folk

Folk Tales with a Caithness Twist

Written by Ian Leith

Illustrated by the pupils of Canisbay Primary School

To Ellen

I. Leith

Baseline Research Ltd

© J. G Leith, 2013

www.baselineresearch.co.uk

ISBN 978-0-9565985-1-6

Printed by Moravian Digital Press, Elgin

Dedicated to the memory of

Anne Mowat

Sister and Teacher

And to Grannies everywhere

Acknowledgements

Folk tales have long been a great pleasure for me. Whether enjoying reading them on my own or re-telling them at storytelling sessions, these magical tales provide an opportunity to dip into a world of fun and wonderment, tempered by their good sense.

In creating these stories I have liberally drawn on many well-known and recognised elements of our folk tales. However I wanted to try to fit them into a Caithness setting, where I first discovered the joy and power of stories.

These tales, I hope can be read and enjoyed by all ages, but I particularly wanted young people to share the enjoyment I get from folk tales. With that in mind, it was agreed that the illustrations should be the work of young people.

I have therefore been privileged to work with the pupils of Canisbay Primary School, who have totally embraced the stories and produced their own unique interpretations of the characters and scenes.

I am also indebted to the management and staff of Canisbay Primary School for their enthusiastic support and co-operation.

In recognition of the above, a percentage of the sale of each copy of this book will go to Canisbay Primary School funds

To my family, I wholeheartedly say a huge thank you. Without their support and forbearance this would not have been possible.

Contents

Granny Clyne
and the Missing Bagpipes

Granny Clyne lived alone in her little cottage, alone, except for her old cat, Topsy. The two of them got on fine together. Granny Clyne would sit in her rocking chair at one side of the fireplace, knitting stockings, while Topsy could usually be found curled up in the old armchair, contentedly purring as she slept. The only time Topsy moved from her comfy spot was to eat her dinner, and to take a daily stroll outside when Granny Clyne went to the shed for coal and peats.

One cold day when all the housework had been done and the fire was stoked up with peats, Granny Clyne settled down to read the latest People's Friend magazine. Topsy was in her usual spot and all was quiet.

After a while Granny Clyne thought she heard a slight knocking noise. At first she just ignored it, but it began to get louder and it seemed to be coming from the cupboard under the kitchen sink.

6

The knocking noise now began to catch the attention of Topsy, who raised one of her eyebrows and had a look on her face that said, "Who is that disturbing me?" Even more worrying for Topsy was when Granny Clyne said to her, "I think we may have a mouse."

The thought of having to get up and start to chase a mouse made the old cat give a disgruntled meow. With the knocking getting even louder it was obvious that if this was a mouse, it must be a very big one. A little bit afraid Granny Clyne slowly opened the cupboard door and there stood, not a mouse, but a funny little man, no more than two feet in height and dressed in a green coloured kilt, a green tweed jacket and a Glengarry bonnet with a small twig of whin attached to it.

Granny Clyne stood back speechless at the sight but the little man stepped out of the cupboard, saying, "What took you so long? I thought I was going to be in there forever."

"Madam," he continued, "I am Wee Sinclair the man who makes sure that all the babies in Caithness grow into beautiful people. It is my task whenever a new baby is born to protect it from being stolen by the fairies and replaced with one of their ugly babies, called changelings. By marching twelve times around the baby's cot in an anti-clockwise direction and playing a set of stirring bagpipe tunes, I can create a place that the fairies cannot reach."

"But what are you doing in my cupboard?" asked Granny Clyne

Wee Sinclair continued in his authoritative voice, "A new baby is expected next door at any time and those troublesome fairies knew I would be in the area so they laid a trap and captured me when you were out for your peats." He continued in an exasperated manner, "They dragged me in here and shut me in this cupboard. But, the worst thing of all is that they have stolen my bagpipes."

Wee Sinclair now complained, "How on earth can I protect the babies if I don't have my bagpipes?"

"Well they cannot be very far away," said Granny Clyne, hopefully. "I'll help you look for them," she said, trying to make Wee Sinclair feel better.

The two of them, Granny Clyne and Wee Sinclair then set about searching for the missing bagpipes. They opened every cupboard, they searched in every nook and cranny, including the shed and the garden, but there was no sign of the bagpipes. Wee Sinclair was now beginning to get and sound desperate.

"What am I to do, what am I to do?" he wailed.

"Let's just stop and think," said Granny Clyne. "I'll make us a cup of tea and we can try to work out what the fairies might have done with your bagpipes." She pulled out a small footstool for Wee Sinclair to sit on and gave him a cup of tea out of a doll's tea set she kept for her grandchildren to play with. There was also some freshly made oatcakes and cheese, which Granny Clyne carefully cut into small sizes for Wee Sinclair.

"You make a fine cup of tea, and these are delicious oatcakes, Granny Clyne," thanked Wee Sinclair, but he was still quite agitated about his missing bagpipes and could not sit still. He jumped off the stool, knocking over his tea and started to pace up and down in front of the fireplace.

"What will I do, what will I do, the baby could come soon and the fairies will steal it away?" His voice was getting louder as he paced and while Granny Clyne tried to reassure him that they would look again, Wee Sinclair was now beginning to get on the nerves of Topsy the cat.

Up until now Topsy had more or less ignored the little man but the voice was now getting in the way of her sleep. At first she opened one eye and gave a wee meow that seemed to say, "Keep the noise down. Can you not see I'm trying to get some sleep?" But Wee Sinclair did not keep the noise down and while Granny Clyne went to tidy away the cups, Topsy thought that maybe if she could stretch out her front leg she might be able to give this horrible noise a biff with her paw. One leg slowly stretched out but it was followed by a strange un-cat like sighing sound! Granny Clyne, who had just returned from the kitchen heard it and thought that the cat was going to be sick. "Come on puss," she called, "Out you go. I'm not having you being sick in here." As Granny Clyne moved towards Topsy, the cat hunched up it's back, as only cats can do. However, before Topsy could get down from the chair an even louder sighing sound emerged from her.

The poor cat was now quite startled by the sounds that she seemed to be making and she leapt out of the chair, knocking Wee Sinclair down as she passed. It was only then that Granny Clyne saw what was making the strange noises. She gleefully lifted Wee Sinclair up to show him what Topsy the cat had been sitting on – his bagpipes!

To say that Wee Sinclair was delighted, well he grabbed the bagpipes and immediately launched into a vigorous set of tunes. Marching around the kitchen table he played like he had never played, while Granny Clyne found new energy to dance a jig. And, such was his skill and joy at being re-united with his bagpipes that he even composed and played a brand new pipe tune, which he called 'The Cat Sat on the Bagpipes'

Later than night when Wee Sinclair had gone, Topsy felt it safe enough to once more go to sleep in the old armchair. As Granny Clyne was preparing to go to bed, the sound of Wee Sinclair's bagpipes drifted through the air and she knew that another new Caithness baby would grow into a handsome boy or girl.

The Haven Brownie

Brownies can be troublesome creatures. It is not their fault it is just their way. Working through the night, under the cover of darkness, lifting, shifting, hiding and tidying, all in the name of being helpful. The Haven Brownie though, went just a wee bit too far.

During the heydays of the Caithness herring fishing, the fishermen from the Haven, and their families, lived in a row of stone built cottages that sat neatly above a natural harbour. The people of the Haven were practical people who knew and respected the mysteries of the seas, and their cottages were their havens sheltering them from the unknown. In the house nearest the harbour road lived John and his wife Lizzie – and a Brownie!

John and Lizzie didn't know they had a Brownie but when Lizzie got up one Friday morning to find pots and dishes in different places from where she had left them the night before, she began to wonder. At first she thought she was maybe going a bit 'dottled' but one night when John was away at the fishing and she was alone in the house she went to bed without tidying up. In the morning all the pots were washed and neatly stacked below the sink, the dishes were arranged in the cupboard and the floor had been scrubbed. Like all country folk, Lizzie had heard of Brownies and now she was certain that somehow she had inherited one. Lizzie also worked out that if she was clever, she could use the Brownie to make life easier for herself. Brownies, you see, cannot resist moving things and most of all they have a compulsion to tidy. Lizzie now went to bed each night without putting away her pots and dishes and in the mornings Lizzie wakened to a clean and tidy house.

This arrangement worked fine for a few weeks but the Brownie began to get bored with its regular routine of cleaning and tidying Lizzie's house. It started to look for ways to expand its field of operations.

It is not possible for a Brownie to ignore the tidying up that has to be done, but there is nothing preventing it from engaging in a bit of mischief.

At first the 'mischief' amounted to little more than putting the sweeping brush in the cupboard with the cups and saucers, and leaving the potty outside the front door, but gradually the Brownie began moving around more and more household items.

The kettle appeared under the bed, the teapot was spotted in the linen cupboard and John's best trousers were lost for a week! None of this seemed to worry Lizzie, she was too happy having someone to do most of her housework.

The Brownie was now having fun and having completed the nightly chores at Lizzie's house he began transferring items, between other houses. The first night it was Lizzie's milk jug that turned up in her neighbour's cupboard. Then over the following nights every house in the row of cottages had an item missing and every house also gained something. A bit of a murmur began between the neighbours about misplaced objects but no one was making too much of it because no one wanted to admit to their neighbours, for fear of being seen as going 'dottled'.

Matters took a turn for the worse though when Lizzie's neighbour, Jessie, found young Barbara from the middle house wearing the brooch that she thought had been misplaced.

The child had simply found this new shiny object in her house and naturally pinned it to her dress. Suddenly there were accusations of thieving children and long-time friends began to fall out - a bad mood settled over the community.

Luckily the mystery was solved the very next night.

Jane, in the house at the opposite end of the row from Lizzie and John, had a new baby and the poor wee mite was suffering from colic. To help comfort the child Jane decided to sit up with her baby and she pulled the rocking chair into a corner beside the fire, made herself and the child comfortable and snuffed out the light. The child eventually quietened and fell asleep while Jane, fearing any movement would wake him again, continued sitting in the rocking chair, enjoying the peaceful darkness.

Then, out of this stillness came a shuffling sound. Jane at first thought it was a mouse but before long the dark outline of something much bigger than a mouse could be seen making its way towards the cupboard.

Afraid of waking and frightening her baby, Jane kept very still and watched as 'something' opened the cupboard, placed an object on a shelf and then removed what Jane recognised, even in this half dark, as her teapot. As the 'thing' turned again towards the door it suddenly stopped and let out a low groan. "Untidy people," it muttered to itself and immediately set about tidying up the bowl and towels Jane had earlier used to bathe the baby. Jane had never encountered a Brownie before but she knew all about their inability to resist tidying.

"So this is the cause of the mischief that has been happening," she said to herself and sat back and watched, from her dark corner, as the housework was done.

Next morning Jane gathered together the rest of the womenfolk and explained what she had discovered. Lizzie was forced to admit that it seemed to be her Brownie, but she agreed with the rest that it needed to be stopped and taught a lesson.

Brownies are very difficult to catch — they are able to slide into spaces where humans cannot reach them. But a very tired Brownie might just let its guard down long enough.

The next evening when everyone went to bed, absolutely no housework had been done during the day. Nothing had been tidied away and nothing had been washed. The Brownie of course was unable to resist the workload and as hoped for, by the time he had reached Jane's house, the last in the line of cottages, he could hardly stand from exhaustion. The women had all gone to bed but none of them had gone to sleep.

As the Brownie tidied and cleaned each house in turn, the women quietly got out of their beds and followed him.

The Brownie sighed and yawned as he put the last of Jane's dishes away in the cupboard and then, without warning, the women pounced and captured the Brownie in a fishing net.

Brownies are not the happiest of creatures, even at the best of times, but a captured Brownie presents a mournful picture. It wept and moaned something piteously, but the women of the Haven knew they had to complete their mission. Taking the lead, Lizzie, together with the other women of the Haven, gathered up the Brownie in the net and carried the unhappy bundle away from the houses and along a moonlit track leading towards a small loch.

The moon sparkled on the water and as he saw where they were heading the Brownie became even more agitated – Brownies cannot swim and have a fear of water. As they drew closer the Brownie pleaded with his captors, that if they would only spare him, he would do anything they asked. This was the moment the women had been waiting for. They had no intention of actually harming the Brownie, but now he was ready to do a deal.

Lizzie agreed that the Brownie belonged in her house and she made sure that she always left him enough chores to keep him busy, although she did sometimes loan him to her neighbours during spring-cleaning time.

The Brownie, he promised to only clean and tidy Lizzie's house, but sometimes that strange shuffling noise can still be heard along the line of cottages, and to this day you will find a house in the vicinity of the Haven that is always spick and span.

Granny Clyne and the Trowie Wife

The night that Granny Clyne was found sitting in the water well with her umbrella held above her head, her family thought she had gone 'clean dottled'.

Actually, Granny Clyne knew exactly what she was doing.

Granny Clyne obviously had not always been a granny. When she was a young woman on her father's croft in Caithness, Catherine Clyne's job was to look after the cows and make sure they were milked twice, every day. At the end of each milking time Catherine did what many other farming and crofter folk did – she left a wee drop of the fresh milk in a hollowed stone that sat outside the byre door. This milk was for the trowies, or as some folk knew them, the fairies.

Trowies are mischievous and troublesome little creatures and can create all kinds of nuisances around the croft. But if they are looked after, they usually keep out of folk's way and can sometimes help with some of the work.

The surest way of keeping on the right side of the trowies is to leave a little fresh milk for them after each milking time. Crofts that do not follow this custom are in danger of finding their cows going dry or the milk going sour.

When Catherine Clyne married and became Catherine MacGregor she and her husband had their own croft and she continued to leave a wee drop of fresh milk for the trowies. However, when Catherine became a mother she had less time to look after some of the outdoor jobs around the croft and, maybe some days, the stone outside the byre was not filled with milk.

After a while, Catherine began to wonder why two of her three cows were producing less milk than normal? Maggie Cow continued to fill the milk pail but Bessie Cow and Jessie Cow were barely filling a milk pail between them. Puzzled by this, Catherine decided to try to find out what was wrong.

Maybe they were not eating enough or perhaps they were eating something that was disagreeing with them.

It was the time of the year when the cows were out on the hillside during the day and Catherine decided that she would go with them to try to discover what was causing their milk problem. So next morning she quietly followed the three cows out to their usual grassy spot. Once they were settled and munching grass and chewing the cud, Catherine crept inside the old ruined croft house that stood close by and settled down to watch. For something to do, and to make sure she stayed alert, Catherine quietly sang some of the songs she had heard sung at the ceilidhs. She was especially keen to try to remember the words of a new song sung at last Friday's ceilidh by one of the bothy lads from the big farm. Bogie's Bonnie Belle he had called it.

> As I gied doon to Huntly toon
>
> Yin morning for to fee
>
> I met wi' Bog o' Cairnie
>
> And him I did agree
>
> To caa his twa best horse and....

...Catherine stopped singing as she sensed that the cows were becoming restless and agitated. Something was unsettling them.

And there it was, coming over the hill track as bold as you like, an old trowie wife.

No more than two feet in height, she was wearing an old tattered green coloured coat and hat and carrying a short gnarled walking stick. The trowie wife marched right up to where Bessie Cow was standing. You would have thought the cow was in a kind of trance, for she just stood there and let the wee trowie wife steal her milk. Jessie Cow also stood stock still, waiting her turn, as though it was the most natural thing in the world.

Maggie Cow, however, had not stood to attention like the others. Instead she had wandered off. Catherine turned to see where she had gone and there she was standing udder deep in a lochan.

The trowie wife had also seen where Maggie had gone and started to dance with rage. Trowies do not like to be outwitted but here was Maggie Cow firmly rooted with water all around her. Trowies will not cross water so there was no way the trowie wife was having any of Maggie's milk. Clattering her stick against a rock the trowie wife stormed away back up the path, muttering some wild sounds as she went.

Next day Catherine again followed the cows out to the hill, waited with them and this time when she saw the trowie wife come down the track, Catherine herded all three cows into the lochan. As you can imagine this did not go down very well with the trowie wife.

When Catherine did the same thing the next day, and the next, the trowie wife finally confronted Catherine. Prodding her with the wee walking stick, Catherine was assured in no uncertain terms that while she may have got the better of the trowie wife for present, she had better look out, for "some day I'll be back." Catherine knew that trowies have long memories.

The three cows returned to providing full milk pails and the trowie wife was not seen near the croft again. In case she was laughed at, Catherine decided not to tell anyone about her encounter with a green-coated trowie wife. She simply carried on as normal, except, that she made sure there was always plenty of milk in the trowie stone outside the byre.

Many years later, and now known to everyone as Granny Clyne, she was living with her son on his farm. She still made sure that a drop of fresh milk was left outside the byre door each day.

People were now less inclined to believe in trowies so Granny Clyne just pretended the milk was for the cats that prowled around the farm.

One night Granny Clyne was alone in the house - everyone else had gone out to the dance in the village hall.

She was sitting in her rocking chair by the window and who should she spy drinking the trowie milk but her old 'friend' with the green coat and hat. Granny Clyne knew that the trowie wife had returned and would try to get even with her. She also knew what she had to do. The lesson that Maggie Cow had taught her, all those years ago, that trowies would not cross water was not forgotten. Granny Clyne quickly left the house, hurried down the path and climbed into the well.

Safe from the trowie wife, Granny Clyne sat there until her family returned and that is why they found her sitting in the well.

As for the umbrella... Well, maybe she was just a wee bit dottled!

The Mermaid's Return

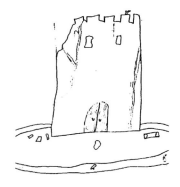

John was an active 11 year-old boy. He went to school and played with his classmates, but he also liked his own company and would often play imaginary games around the cottage at Noss in Caithness, where he lived with his mother and father.

The family had once included a daughter, Susan, but she had died in a drowning accident some years ago. John was only about three years old at the time and remembered little of the incident. His mother and father never talked about Susan, and John assumed that they had moved to the North of Scotland to help them forget.

John's active imagination was fuelled by his passion for books and he would find himself creating his own imaginary exciting and daring adventures. His favourite place for these daydream exploits was the ruined Sinclair Castle that imposed itself on the view from John's bedroom window. On bright sunny mornings the shadows from its stones would create patterns across the fields and on misty days it would appear and disappear out of the gloom. Only a fraction of this once mighty stronghold remained. John was forbidden by his father to go anywhere near the crumbling structure. Left to imagine himself as the hero of the fortress, John could only do so at a distance.

One Saturday, John's parents had an appointment in Inverness and John asked if he might stay at home instead of having to endure the long car journey. His mother said that as he had his homework to complete, he could stay at home. She would arrange with their neighbour, Mrs Ross, to keep an eye on him. John's father was reluctant, but eventually he was persuaded and gave in. They departed on the Saturday morning, leaving a host of dire warnings for John should he think about getting up to anything.

John however was an obedient boy and once his parents had departed he sat down to his homework and at twelve o clock he went next door to Mrs Ross. She had not only agreed to look out for John but to also provide his lunch. John eagerly tucked in to the bowl of lentil soup, a plate of mince and tatties, followed by two plates of trifle, while Mrs Ross prattled on about nothing in particular. John was not too sure what to do once lunch was over – was he to stay with Mrs Ross, or could he go back to his own home? Mrs Ross however liked to have a nap after lunch, so it was on her suggestion that John could go out to play and pop round again later for some afternoon tea.

John agreed and thanked Mrs Ross for his lunch and headed down the garden path. There in front of him stood the top tier of Sinclair Castle. What harm if he was just to go a wee bit closer? He could really do with seeing a bit more of it – the story in his head at the moment had the hero fighting off some Viking intruders and he needed to know if the Viking raiders could have rowed their boats up to the castle.

As the story of the Vikings took over John's thoughts, he was unaware of just how close he was to the old ruin. John had in fact reached a point where he could see down and across the grassy hill that led to the castle's entrance. What John did not see was the rabbit hole that engulfed his foot.

One minute John was imagining a group of Viking warriors clambering out of their boat and rushing towards the castle. The next he was tumbling head over heels down the hill. Fortunately, the landing was soft and grassy. As he picked himself up, unhurt, he was sure he heard the sound of a 'plop' in the waters of the geo.

No one could be seen, but sure enough there were circular ripples in the water – the kind you get if someone throws a pebble into the water. In John's now highly charged excitement, the possibility of someone else being there made him dash heroically in through the castle entrance.

Inside it was dark and a bit smelly but John, now that he had entered the stronghold, was not about to give up the chance to explore. He tried to make a mental picture of the layout to take away with him. The next instalment of his story was already forming in his head. His detailed search first found the entrance to what must be the dungeon but it was too dark to venture in. The remains of what may have been some stairs snaked up the remaining stone built walls. Much of the castle wall had long ago fallen down but John guessed that somewhere there would be a way down to the sea, and sure enough, only a few feet from the dungeon steps, there was a large hole in the floor.

Looking down through the hole, John could clearly see the stone steps leading downwards, but unlike the way down to a dark dungeon these steps were lit by daylight.

Nothing was going to stop John completing a full exploration now, so down the steps he went. As he reappeared from the bottom of the hole into the full glare of the sunlight his eyes were drawn towards a mass of shimmering colours. Every colour, to be found in the sea, sparkled up to him from a big flat rock and there sitting with her back to John was a young woman with golden hair cascaded over her upper body, while the profusion of colour formed her lower half. John stood awestruck! Afraid to move for fear of disturbing her he was also unable to speak because the words that came into his head refused to leave his mouth.

"Come and sit beside me John," is what his head told him he heard. Not until the words were repeated, and this glorious creature turned round to face him, was his trance broken.

Somewhat startled, John asked, "You know my name?"

"Yes John, I know you, just as I knew you would come here one day," was the reply.

As John slowly drew near to the big rock he stuttered, "You are a... Mermaid? "Do you live here? Are there other mermaids here? I must go home."

"You are safe with me John," her soft and gentle voice reassured him enough to permit him to sit down close by.

She continued, "Yes, I am a mermaid and I regularly come here because I am searching for my mother. My mother is desperate to join me, but she is prevented from doing so because she is held captive by a man."

"Is she locked up somewhere?" asked John. "Maybe I could help you cut her free." His mind had returned to swashbuckling mode and John's imaginary tales of adventure envisioned this mermaid's mother trapped in an underwater cage.

"Unfortunately my mother is not trapped in a cage," sighed the mermaid. "She is a prisoner in a human body."

"How?" was all John was able to reply.

The mermaid began to tell her tale. "It happened like this."

"One day my mother was sitting on a rock, just as I am. The sun was shining so she slipped away from the other merfolk to enjoy some peace and quiet. Suddenly a big strong young man grabbed her from behind. You have to be very strong to be able to hold on to a mermaid – we are quite slippery!"

"Anyway," she continued, "this man was strong enough to drag this very frightened mermaid up the beach and away from the sea. She pleaded to let him return to her own people and offered him the mermaid's three wishes if he would let her go."

"Mermaids have the power to grant humans three wishes and when the third is granted she is released. This strong young man knew about this power of the merfolk and had obviously planned it well."

"I will ask my wishes," he said. "One today, a second sometime in the future, but the third I will not seek until I am on my dying bed. Only then will you be free."

"What do you want of me?" the distraught mermaid cried. "Me and my people have done you no harm."

"I have watched you for days and weeks," replied the young man. "Your beauty has bewitched me. So I have decided to make you my wife. Mermaid, grant me my first wish – I wish us to be married."

"So the young man brought his new wife to live with him. He was married to the prettiest woman in the village. She however was the saddest woman in that village," explained the mermaid.

John sat engrossed and thoughtful at the mermaid's side before asking, "Didn't people think it strange to see a mermaid among them?"

His mermaid companion laughed and said, "Mermaids have many powers John, and one of them is to take the shape of what is around them. To humans she appeared as a woman, but inside she was still a mermaid and ached to be back in the ocean." To relieve the silence that now descended, John asked, "Did the man ask her for his second wish?"

"Oh yes, he asked and was granted his second wish," she replied. "His second wish was that she would provide him with a family. First a girl was born and then some seven years later a boy.

When the mother considered the girl old enough to fully understand her story, she found an excuse for the two of them to be out of the house on their own. The man was always very strict about them being alone together but one day she saw, and took her chance."

John was fast working out some of the mystery. "So the girl was you?"

"Yes, that day, seven years ago, my mother took me by the hand down to the beach where she told me her story and then began singing in a voice that I had never heard before. In time, her song was answered from out at sea and it was then that she made me walk into the waves."

"At first I could not work out what was happening, but slowly, ever so slowly, I began to change from human to mermaid. All the time I was being drawn to this magical singing from the sea. That was the day I went to live with the merfolk. My mother was unable to come with me because of the three wishes, but she sent me instead."

Sadly, John asked, "Have you never seen her since then?"

"No," she sighed, "but I know she is becoming desperate. She has been out of the sea too long already and must return soon, if she is not to die on land. Her powers will be getting weaker and she will not always be able to appear in human form."

John worked back through the story, trying to piece it all together "What happened to the boy?" he enquired

"Oh he is well for the present," replied the mermaid.

"What happened to the family?" John's mind was working overtime.

"You already know the answer to that John," and with one quick swish of her tail, the mermaid brought them both into the water. "It has taken me a long time to lure you to me, John. I do not intend to hurt you, for you are my brother, but you are the only hope I have of releasing my mother."

"She is my mother too!" shouted John, "why should I lose her?"

Now very wet and cold, John asked somewhat fearfully, "What are you going to do with me?"

"I will take you to a cave under the castle where it is dry and safe," she assured him. "There we will wait for mother and father to come."

How long he was there John could not tell, but after what seemed like a long time his sister, the mermaid, re-appeared.

"They are approaching now," she informed him.

"How did you know they would look here for me?" quizzed John.

"You asked if I had ever seen my mother again and truly I have not, but we have a means of communicating. She knows I am here and she will have worked out that you are here with me," she answered with confidence.

Before long, John could hear his father's voice calling his name. He tried to call back but the sound just bounced back and echoed around the walls of the cave.

"We will go and sit on a rock at the side of the geo," his sister instructed. "They will see us from there. Do not make a sound or attempt to move." Her order was given in that authoritative tone, John recognised as his father's.

Now, perched together on the rock, the human boy and the mermaid girl watched as their parents ran down the hillside.

"Let him go!" shouted their father. "He belongs with me, here on the land."

"You shall have him father, but only when you release my mother," came the reply.

"Please!" pleaded their mother. "She will not harm him if you let me go. Ask me for one more wish and John will be at your side."

The man could see he was beaten. If he refused he would lose both of his children.

Reluctantly, for in his own way he loved his wife, and the thought of not seeing her again was hard to imagine. He cried, "I wish for my son to be returned to me"

There was a great splashing of water and when he had wiped his eyes, John found himself standing at the water's edge beside his father. Of the mermaids, all that could be seen were two circles of ripples in the water.

John and his father watched the circles grow smaller and smaller, then trudged slowly home, their hearts heavy with sadness, tears stinging their eyes and not a word between them. In the eyes of their neighbours, another tragic drowning had befallen the family and again they moved home. Every year John returns to Sinclair Castle and sits waiting, knowing that his sister will eventually come back. He sits on the big flat rock and waits for Susan to arrive. He tells her of his world and she promises to pass it on to their mother.

"Oh by the way, Susan, how did you know I would be returned to my father and not join you and mother?" John asked.

"You are a male child, only female children of a man and mermaid union retain the genes of the merfolk," she replied.

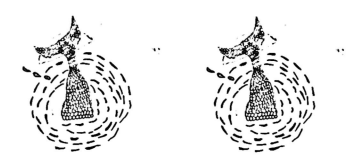

A Meteor at Ackergill

(Adapted from a story told by Hugh Miller in Scenes and Legends)

About the year 1650, Oliver Cromwell's armies were fighting the Royalists in Scotland and it was common for ships to be used to transport the soldiers around the coasts. One of these ships was bound for Caithness and sailed up the east coast of Scotland with a cargo of Cromwell's soldiers. The plan was to land at Wick but when they arrived there was such a strong westerly wind blowing that the ship could make no headway in towards the mouth of the Wick River.

The ship's captain was therefore forced to make the decision to steer his vessel and its cargo around Noss Head and into the relative calm of Sinclair Bay. Here they dropped anchor just off the imposing Ackergill Tower. At this point the ship's crew were able to ferry the soldiers into the little harbour at Ackergill. From there it was an easy three-mile march to Wick.

The ship and its crew had been at sea for some time so the Captain decided that his men deserved a rest. The Captain, along with two volunteers, remained on board while the other sailors were allowed to accompany the soldiers into the town, on the understanding that they would return, ready to sail 48 hours later.

That night when his two shipmates had gone to sleep, the Captain strolled onto the deck, took out his pipe and sat down under the night sky.

The lights from the houses around the bay flickered through the darkness and the Captain watched them go out, one by one, until only one small illumination remained. As the Captain's pipe went out, this last speck of light also disappeared into the night's darkness.

Almost immediately it had been extinguished there came a strange hissing noise from above. Looking upwards, the Captain saw a meteor arc through the sky and speed downwards to where that last light had been seen. The glowing brightness from the falling missile lit up a single cottage and somewhere a dog howled, while an owl gave a long eerie hoot.

As the meteor continued its downward trajectory the captain could only stare and wait for it to crash into the roof of the cottage. Then, just as the meteor was only a few feet above the building, from somewhere, a cockerel crowed. Coming to a sudden halt the meteor hovered over the cottage for a few minutes before slowly climbing back up into the night sky.

When this burning 'skyrocket' had regained some considerable height it began to arc downwards again, once more towards the cottage. Once more the cock crowed and the meteor's descent was halted. Again it hovered before slowly rising into the sky. On the third attack the Captain could feel a real menace in the sound and speed as it approached the cottage. This time from inside the cottage came the sound of wings flapping furiously and an accompanying sound that the Captain could only describe as a defiant bird noise. This time the meteor halted before drifting back up into the stars.

In all his long days and the many places he had visited, the Captain had never encountered anything like this, and here was a man who was well accustomed to studying the night sky.

The next night and intrigued by this phenomena the Captain took up the same position on the deck. Again he watched as the sprinkling of lights from the houses around the bay, were extinguished. Again, the same cottage light was the last one to be snuffed. The Captain could only stare in amazement and disbelief as once more the meteor reappeared, hurtling towards the same lonely cottage.

The dog howled and the owl hooted and following a repeat of the previous night's exchange between cockerel and meteor, the latter retreated back into the heavens.

Next morning the Captain rose early and rowed ashore determined to find and visit the site of this nightly battle between a sky demon and some form of feathered defendant. The Captain made his way in the direction of the cottage and coming over a small hill, there below him stood a roughly built stone dwelling.

The cottage turned out to be the home of an old wife who looked at the Captain as if he were mad when he asked about the commotion he had witnessed. The old woman said that she lived alone in the cottage, with only her dog to keep her company and an old cockerel to wake her in the mornings. Seeing the woman had nothing much in the way of food or clothing the Captain thought he could help her by offering to buy the cockerel – for surely this was no ordinary bird. The old woman was delighted with the price offered and was glad to be rid of the "scrawny old thing." With the deal concluded, the Captain, carrying the cockerel under his arm, returned to his ship.

When the ship's crew had returned, and with cockerel included, the ship set sail for its next destination.

About a month later this same ship returned to Sinclair Bay. This time the mission was to uplift the soldiers and transport them on to their next operation.

The cockerel during this time had lived on the ship and had become fat on the titbits the captain and the crew threw its way. No meteors had been seen and the bird behaved exactly as cockerels do – crowing at sunrise and eating and strutting the rest of the time.

The Captain decided that since he was back in Ackergill he would give the now fat bird, back to the old woman. Maybe she could sell it again for a good price. So he made his way along the track to the cottage - but there was no cottage to be seen and when he arrived at the spot, all that existed was a pile of blackened stones.

The people of Ackergill assured the Captain that the cottage had been unoccupied for a year or more, but they told him that on the very night he had last sailed out of the bay, the cottage had mysteriously burst into flames.

the woman

cockerel   Dog

Granny Clyne
and the Groatie Buckie

Granny Clyne was on her holidays. Each year she spent two weeks looking after her granddaughter. Margaret was eight this year and she was particularly excited because this was the year Granny Clyne had promised to go looking for Groatie Buckies.

The best place to find Groatie Buckies is along the seashore between John O'Groats and Duncansby Head. Here if you are very careful and lucky you may find one of these tiny shells nestling among the sandy shoreline. Margaret had never found one yet but she was sure that if she went with Granny Clyne they would be certain to find a first Groatie Buckie. Granny Clyne had a jar at home containing quite a few Groatie Buckies she had collected over the years. Margaret intended to start her own collection.

As soon as Granny Clyne arrived at Margaret's house she was being asked "when would they be going shell hunting?" Granny Clyne promised that next morning they would make a start.

Margaret's house was a few miles from John O'Groats, so the next day Granny and Margaret walked to the end of the farm road where they would catch the bus. It was like many days in Caithness, windy and a little cold, so Granny Clyne wore her warm jumper and a bright red fleecy lined jacket. Margaret too was kitted out in a red duffle coat, red welly boots, red scarf and red gloves. Granny Clyne said she looked just like Little Red Riding Hood.

Before setting out on their search, Granny Clyne and Margaret visited the John O'Groats café where they each had a mug of steaming hot chocolate. Now, warm inside and out, they set off along the shoreline. With their heads bent against the wind and their eyes focused on looking for Groatie Buckies, neither of them was aware of the big black dog bounding towards them. Just in time Granny Clyne looked up and was able to lift Margaret out of its path. The dog at first seemed to have ignored them. Then it suddenly stopped and turned, throwing up a storm of sand as it did so. The animal took a long look at Granny Clyne before quietly coming forward and gently laying down in the sand, a bright red object.

"Look, Margaret, the doggie has brought us his ball," said Granny Clyne.

"I don't think it's a ball, Granny," replied Margaret as she bent down to pick up the strange object. "Look its got shells stuck to it," she said as she handed it to Granny Clyne.

"My word, you are right. But these are not shells, they are some kind of jewels," said Granny Clyne as she looked in wonder at this magnificent ball. "I wonder where the dog found it?"

So fascinated were Granny Clyne and Margaret that they had not noticed the dog bound away along the shore. Yet in no time at all, the dog was back at their feet, this time with another shiny object. Now, dangling from the dog's mouth was what looked like a bracelet. No sooner had Granny Clyne picked this up, than he was off again and returned now with a small tiara. Before the dog could run away again, Granny Clyne grabbed hold of him. "I think we had better follow this dog," suggested Granny Clyne to Margaret.

"When I let him go, you run after him, Margaret," instructed Granny Clyne. "At my age I'm no very good at running. You see if you can find out where the doggie is finding these magnificent items."

Margaret set off after the dog and had not gone very far along the shore when she caught up with the dog, nose first in a hole in the sand. The dog had unearthed an old wooden chest and Margaret could see that inside were more shiny and sparkling objects. As Margaret hauled the box out of the sandy hole, Granny Clyne arrived, a bit out of breath.

"It's buried treasure," exclaimed Margaret, excitedly. "Do you think these things are old, Granny?"

"Oh yes," replied Granny Clyne. "I think they may be very old."

As the two of them examined the contents of the chest, they found a brooch, a number of rings and a piece of parchment tightly rolled up inside a glass bottle.

"Maybe this belonged to a princess, Granny," said Margaret hopefully. She often dressed up and pretended to be a princess.

In her mind with these items she would now look the part. "Can I keep some pieces, Granny?" asked Margaret.

Granny Clyne was not really listening. She was too engrossed in what was written on the piece of parchment. The words were obviously not in English but Granny Clyne could understand one phrase,

'Margaret, datter av kong Eric II'

"Margaret we must put these things back in this box," Granny Clyne said very seriously. "I think

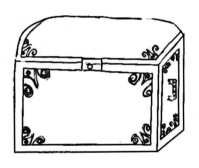 these items did indeed once belong to a princess."

"We should sit here and have our lunch-time sandwich, and I'll tell you a story about a princess from long ago."

As Granny Clyne unpacked the sandwiches she began to tell of how many years ago a King of Scotland fell from his horse and died, without having any children of his own. The lords and important men of Scotland decided that the next heir to the Scottish throne should be the King's granddaughter. She however lived in Norway, where her father was also a King.

An agreement was reached between the two countries and this Norwegian princess was made ready to sail for Scotland.

"You will never guess what her name was," asked Granny Clyne. Margaret guessed at a few names she thought might be a good princess name – "Catherine?", no. "Guinevere?", no, and so on until Margaret remembered that if she was a Norwegian princess, she would have a Norwegian name. "Ingrid or Astrid?

"No," said Granny Clyne, "her name was Margaret, same as you."

"Wow, I'm named after a real princess. What happened to Princess Margaret, Granny?"

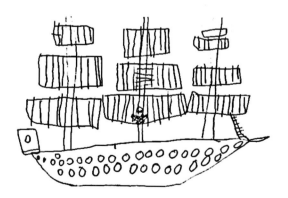

"Well," continued Granny Clyne, "its not a very happy ending I'm afraid. Margaret, who was known as the Maid of Norway, was put on a ship in Norway bound for Scotland. Unfortunately, she became terribly sea sick and ill when the ship was caught up in a wild storm. The ship was due to land at the Port of Leith, but because of the weather it headed instead for the Orkney Islands. When it eventually landed, the Maid of Norway was so ill that she died at the place now known as St. Margaret's Hope."

"This box that we have found may well be the jewels of The Maid of Norway," said Granny Clyne sadly. "Whether they were washed overboard in the storm, or deliberately thrown overboard so that they would not find their way into the hands of the Lords of Scotland, nobody will know. But my guess is that the box has been floating about in the Pentland Firth, before finally being washed ashore here. Over the years it has been covered by lots of sand and here it remained until today when the doggie showed it to us."

"Where is the doggie, Granny?" asked Margaret.

"I expect he has gone away home," answered Granny Clyne, but she was also sure it was no ordinary dog. Somehow it had been sent to show them this box of treasure.

"What will we do with this treasure box, Granny?" asked Margaret, hoping that she would say that Margaret could add it to her dressing up box.

"We must take it to the National Museum of Scotland as soon as possible. This is important stuff, Margaret," said Granny Clyne seriously.

So the two of them gathered up all their belongings, tucked the treasure chest in the lunch basket and set off for home.

Later that night when Margaret's parents arrived home, the treasure discovery was explained and the treasure chest emptied out on the kitchen table. Margaret's Dad said he would contact the Museum first thing in the morning. That night Margaret's dreams were all about being dressed in fine jewels and sailing on a fine ship.

Next day, Granny Clyne and Margaret spent quite a long time searching the Internet for information about the Maid of Norway. Margaret noted down all of the facts so that she could tell her teacher and her classmates when they returned to school.

Every now and again Granny Clyne would drift away into a kind of trance as she too thought about the young Maid of Norway.

Just after lunchtime there came a knock at the door. Margaret ran to answer it to find two men in dark suits, with briefcases, asking to speak with her Dad. "We are from the National Museum of Scotland," they announced. Margaret proudly said that it was herself and her Granny they needed to talk to as they had found the Maid of Norway's jewels.

The two men were at first quite off-hand about the find but became quite excited when Granny showed them the box and its contents. When they read the words on the piece of parchment they began to talk very loudly and Margaret was sure one of them actually jumped up and down.

After a while the men left with the box of jewels, giving Granny Clyne a receipt to say that the items were now in the custody of the National Museum. Just before they left, one of the men turned and handed something to Margaret. "Oh you can keep this piece that was lying in the bottom of the box. I don't think this would have been part of the collection."

Margaret stared down at the thing in her hand. It was a Groatie Buckie.

Margaret had forgotten all about the Groatie Buckie hunt and now she had one to start her collection.

"I think these men are wrong, Margaret," said Granny Clyne. "That shell was deliberately put in that box to keep it safe. It is a well known fact around here, that if you keep a Groatie Buckie in your purse you will never run out of money."

Granny Clyne (the song)
(To the tune of The Quartermaster's Store.)

While working on the illustrations for these stories, the pupils of Canisbay Primary School wrote this Granny Clyne song

Chorus (repeat after each verse)

Her eyes are dim, she cannot see.

She has a cat upon her knee.

She has a cat upon her knee.

Verse 1

She is kind, kind, her name is Granny Clyne.

Granny Clyne, Granny Clyne.

She is kind, kind, her name is Granny Clyne.

Her name is Granny Clyne.

Verse 2

There was a knock, knock, gave Granny Clyne a shock.

What a shock, what a shock!

There was a knock, knock, gave Granny Clyne a shock.

Granny Clyne got a great big shock!

Verse 3

Out came Sinclair, Sinclair, was stuck under the sink there.

Poor wee Sinclair, poor wee Sinclair!

Out came Sinclair, Sinclair, was stuck under the sink there.

Sinclair was stuck under the sink!

Verse 4

He was small, small, he was only 2 feet tall.

2 feet tall, 2 feet tall!

He was small, small, he was only 2 feet tall.

Sinclair was 2 feet tall!

Verse 5

He was a man, man, he could barely stand.

Barely stand, barely stand!

He was a man, man, he could barely stand.

Wee Sinclair could barely stand!

Verse 6

He plays the pipes, pipes, to give fairies a fright!

What a fright, what a fright!

He plays the pipes, pipes, to give fairies a fright!

The fairies get a fright!

Verse 7

The pipes were there, there, on Granny Clyne's armchair!

Her armchair, her armchair.

The pipes were there, there, on Granny Clyne's armchair!

They were on the old armchair!